D0261308

STAFFORDSHIRE LIBRARY AND INFORMATION SERVICES
Please return or renew by the last date shown

		BURTON LIBRARY HIGH ST BUTON-ON-TRENT TEL: 239556 CHILDREN'S LIBRARY
14. MAY 12		

If not required by other readers, this item may be renewed in person, by post or telephone, online or by email.
To renew, either the book or ticket are required

24 HOUR RENEWAL LINE 0845 33 00 740

STAFFORDSHIRE LIBRARIES

3 8014 09246 6801

For Milo Lorcan and Augusta

First published 2012 by Walker Books Ltd
87 Vauxhall Walk, London SE11 5HJ

2 4 6 8 10 9 7 5 3 1

© 2012 Jessica Spanyol

The right of Jessica Spanyol to be identified as author/illustrator of
this work has been asserted by her in accordance with the
Copyright, Designs and Patents Act 1988.

This book has been typeset in TypographyofCoop

Printed in China

All rights reserved. No part of this book may be reproduced, transmitted or
stored in an information retrieval system in any form or by any means, graphic,
electronic or mechanical, including photocopying, taping and recording,
without prior written permission from the publisher.

British Library Cataloguing in Publication Data:
a catalogue record for this book is available
from the British Library.

ISBN 978-1-4063-3418-0

www.walker.co.uk

MY MUM is BEAUTiFUL

JESSICA SPANYOL

WALKER BOOKS
AND SUBSIDIARIES
LONDON · BOSTON · SYDNEY · AUCKLAND

My Mum is beautiful because she likes my pictures.

My Mum is beautiful because she helps me sweep up.

My Mum is beautiful because she has my toys in her bath.

My Mum is beautiful because she lets me jump in puddles.

My Mum is beautiful because she has tea with teddy.

My Mum is beautiful because she snuggles up with me.

My Mum is beautiful because she takes me to the café.

My Mum is beautiful because we go shopping together.

My Mum is beautiful because she feeds the ducks with me.

My Mum is beautiful because she laughs when I wear her slippers.

My Mum is beautiful because she really loves me.

My Mum is the most beautiful
Mum in the whole world.